Vol.5

WANN

Give to the Heart Vol. 5

Story and Art by WANN

Produced by Ecomix Media Company
Translator Jeong Lee
Editor Philip Daay
Graphic Designer Jihye Kim, Heejong Lee, purj
Publisher Heewoon Chung

5405 Wilshire Blvd. Suite 269
Los Angeles, CA 90036
info@netcomics.com
www.NETCOMICS.com

ISBN: 978-1-60009-956-4
First printing: September 2015
10 9 8 7 6 5 4 3 2 1
Printed in Korea

Give to the Heart

Vol.5

WANN

YOU'RE QUIET FOR A NOMAD. THEY'RE USUALLY PRETTY TALKATIVE.
HERE, EAT UP. YOU LOOK HUNGRY.
YOU DON'T EVEN CARRY TRAVEL BAGS.
AH...
OH MY... YOU MUST HAVE BEEN ROBBED DURING YOUR JOURNEYS!
AT LEAST, YOU FOUND YOUR WAY TO OUR PEACEFUL TOWN.
YOU COULD'VE ENDED UP DEAD ON THE ROAD!
UM, DAD...
YOU'RE RIGHT. I SHOULD LEAVE HIM IN PEACE.
HE CAN'T EAT IF I KEEP YAPPING HIS EAR OFF.
SET UP A BED FOR HIM IN THE HALL BEDROOM.
OKAY.
...

OH NO. I STACKED OUR BUSHELS OF FLOUR IN THERE.
SHE'LL HAVE A HARD TIME MOVING THEM.
I'LL HELP HER.
HAA
HAA
AH...!
SLIP
GRAB
AH...
PLOP
PLOP
PLOP
PLOP

THE HIGH AND MIGHTY WATER KING GETS HIS HANDS DIRTY JUST LIKE US MERE MORTALS.
...
SHOULD I JUST WATCH YOU WORK THEN?
WHY ARE YOU HERE?
...
STOP
I WAS DOING FINE.
I WAS DOING PERFECTLY FINE WITHOUT YOU.
I... FINALLY...
WHY ARE YOU HERE!

YOU'RE DOING FINE...
I SEE, YOU'RE DOING FINE.
THAT'S ALL I WANTED TO HEAR.
I'M SATISFIED NOW.
TELL YOUR FATHER I'LL LEAVE EARLY IN THE MORNING.
HEY!

...
GOOD... BYE.
SLAM
...
TOSS TURN
FLIP FLOP
HAA

I JUST...

...CAN'T SLEEP.

OH...
I COULDN'T WAIT UNTIL MORNING, AFTER ALL. I INTEND TO LEAVE RIGHT NOW.
...

LEAVE?
...

...
WHY...
...DID YOU NEED TO SHOW YOUR FACE TO ME?
THMP
DAMN IT!

UBT
PANG
PANG
UBT

W...
HAA
UBT

SLAM
THUD
HAA
Q-QUIET...
DAD WILL FIND US!
HAA
THUD
HAA
AHH!

AHH...
KREEK
HAA
KREEK
AHH...
AHHH

KREEK
AHHH
KREEK
KREEK
KREEK
KREEK
UH... GH
KREEK
KREEK
AHH...
KRRRRNG
TAP

HAA
THUD
GANOK...

HAA
HAA
I WAS... GOING TO LEAVE.
I SWEAR.
HAA
SLIP
HAA
...
...

I ADMIT, AT FIRST,
I INTENDED TO TAKE YOU
BACK EVEN IF IT MEANT
KIDNAPPING YOU.
...
...
YOU...
MISSED ME?

...
BE TRUTHFUL.
DID YOU MISS ME?
CREAK
DO YOU THINK I CAME HERE BECAUSE OF BOREDOM?
ARE YOU TRYING TO GUESS MY WEAKNESSES?
I JUST WANTED TO SEE YOU.
SO, DON'T TRY TO FIGURE OUT MY WEAKNESSES!
...

YOU'RE SO UPTIGHT. SO VERY UPTIGHT.
IS TELLING A WOMAN THAT YOU LIKE HER A WEAKNESS?
THEN, I GUESS I'M BRAVER THAN YOU.
I MISSED YOU.
I ACTUALLY MISSED YOU, YOU SON OF A BITCH!
HAA
I NEVER HAD A CHOICE WITH YOU.

HUH? WHAT ARE YOU SAYING?
I CAN'T HELP MYSELF ANYMORE.
IT'S TOO LATE FOR YOU TO SAY NO.
LIVE WITH ME.
GIVE ME THE REST OF YOUR LIFE.
I WANT YOUR ALL. ALL YOUR REMAINING YEARS.
GANOK...

I CAN'T LOVE YOU THE WAY HUMAN MEN DO.
I CAN'T SHARE MY ALL WITH YOU EITHER.
I POSSESS MANY SECRETS. YOU WOULDN'T BE ABLE TO UNDERSTAND ME EVEN IF YOU KNEW THEM.
ALSO...
...I THINK I WILL MAKE LOVE WITH YOU UNTIL YOU CAN'T EVEN STAND ANYMORE.
STILL...
WHAT ARE YOU DOING?!
SLAM

DAD!
YOU RUFFIAN!
HAVE YOU NO DECENCY? HOW DARE YOU TAKE ADVANTAGE OF A HOST'S DAUGHTER?
AH!
DAD! NO!
YOU DON'T UNDERSTAND!

WHAT ARE YOU SAYING?
HAA
YOU WANTED HIM?
BECAUSE HE'S A NOMAD?
ARE YOU SAYING YOU "BORROWED" HIM?
...
YOU WERE NEVER INTERESTED IN THAT PRACTICE.
HE'S NOT A NOMAD!
WHAT IS HE THEN?
WELL... HE IS... HE IS...
RUMBLE
KRMPH

HEY! LAHOON!
SOME TOWNSFOLK SAW A STRANGE YOUNG MAN ENTER YOUR HOME.
HOUSEHOLDS WITH YOUNG DAUGHTERS SHOULDN'T BE HOSTING NOMADS!
WOMEN HAVE THE RIGHT TO BORROW NOMADS...
...BUT MEN HAVE THE RIGHT TO TEACH SUCH NOMADS A LESSON!
SOMETIMES NOMADS ARE KILLED BY ANGRY MOBS WHO HATE THE PRACTICE OF BORROWING.
BUT, THAT HAS NEVER HAPPENED IN THIS TOWN BEFORE.
WE DON'T WISH TO CAUSE YOU TROUBLE!
JUST HAND OVER THE NOMAD!
NONSENSE!
YOU'RE GOING TO KILL HIM JUST BECAUSE HE'S A NOMAD?
WE DON'T WANT HIM HERE SEDUCING OUR WOMEN!

HAS SOOYI ALREADY FALLEN FOR HIM?
ARGHH
...
WE HAVE NO DESIRE TO TEAR DOWN YOUR HOUSE, BUT IF YOU INSIST ON PROTECTING HIM...

...
STAND
WHERE ARE YOU GOING?

IF I DON'T GO OUTSIDE, THEY'LL DESTROY YOUR HOME.

I CAN'T FORGIVE YOU FOR TOUCHING SOOYI, BUT THAT DOESN'T MEAN I'LL SEND YOU OUT TO DIE!

YOU WON'T BE ABLE TO FORGIVE ME FOR OTHER REASONS.
WHAT DO YOU MEAN?

GANOK!
THERE HE IS!
THE NOMAD!
HAHA... HE LOOKS QUITE TALL AND BUILT FOR A NOMAD.
HE DOESN'T LOOK SCARED AT ALL.
LET'S SEE HOW TALL HE STANDS AFTER WE BREAK HIS ARMS AND LEGS!
STOP IT!

WHAT ARE YOU ALL DOING?
IF YOU'RE HERE TO LECTURE US, GET LOST!
YOU CAN'T EVEN PROTECT YOUR OWN GIRL!
FLIP
MOVE OUT OF THE WAY!
HOW COULD YOU ALL ATTACK A NOMAD? THAT'S UNFORGIVABLE!
UGH...!
SLIDE
...
LET GO OF ME!
NO! DON'T GO OUTSIDE.
IT'S NOT THE NOMAD I'M WORRIED ABOUT!

PWOOM
AAAK
SOO...
SLAM
GANOK, STOP!
THOSE ARE MY TOWNSPEOPLE! DON'T HURT...

STAY CALM.
I MERELY TAUGHT THEM A TINY LESSON.
I INFLICTED MERE SCRATCHES, SO RELAX.
JUST WHO... ARE YOU?
WHO ARE YOU?!!!
AH...
...
THE WATER KING!

THE WATER KING?
CHATTER
UGH...
ARE YOU TRYING TO TAKE SOOYI AGAIN, WATER KING?
REEL
SHE IS NEITHER YOUR TOY NOR YOUR SLAVE!
AND WHAT IF I DID TAKE HER?
YOU THINK THESE TERRIFIED IDIOTS WILL STOP ME?
SURELY, THEY WOULD SACRIFICE ONE LITTLE GIRL FOR THE SAKE OF PROTECTING THEIR TOWN. AM I CORRECT?
IF YOU DARE TOUCH SOOYI...

SHUT UP, NARIGA!
ARE YOU TRYING TO GET US ALL KILLED?
YES, YOU ARE RIGHT.
SHE IS NEITHER MY TOY NOR MY SLAVE.
BESIDES, I CAN'T STAND HUMANS THINKING OF HER THAT WAY.
IF I DO TAKE HER, SHE'LL BE GIVEN A POSITION SO HIGH THAT NO ONE WOULD DARE LOOK DOWN ON HER AGAIN.
SHE WILL BE MY QUEEN, THE WIFE OF THE WATER KING.

WHAT...
...DID HE JUST SAY?
HUMAN LAWS, CUSTOMS AND TITLES MEAN NOTHING TO ME...
...BUT SOMETIMES IT'S SIMPLER TO JUST COOPERATE WITH THEM.
I DON'T WISH TO CAUSE MORE PROBLEMS BY LIVING WITH SOOYI WITHOUT A HUMAN MARRIAGE CEREMONY.
YOU CAN'T JUST COME HERE AND DO WHATEVER YOU WANT!
OF COURSE, I CAN.
I'VE ALREADY GIVEN SOOYI A PROPOSAL OF SORTS.
SHE HASN'T GIVEN ME AN ANSWER, THOUGH I PROBABLY WOULDN'T HONOR HER REFUSAL ANYWAY.

SHE IS NOW... MINE.
NOW, ALL OF YOU...
...FIX EVERYTHING THAT YOU BROKE.
GRAB
KRMPPP

KLING
BRMM
BRMM
BRMM

HISTORIANS SAY THIS WAS THE FIRST TIME IN HISTORY THAT THE WATER KING TOOK A WIFE.
THE PEOPLE OF HASOOMAL WERE THROWN INTO CHAOS.
THEIR INSIGNIFICANT LITTLE TOWN WAS ABOUT TO BECOME THE HOME CITY OF THE WATER QUEEN.
BURIED UNDERNEATH THE FANCIFUL WEDDING CELEBRATION, COMPLICATED POLITICAL DEVELOPMENTS PLAYED OUT.
RULERS OF LARGE AND SMALL CITIES SENT VALUABLE GIFTS.
THE TOWN RECEIVED MORE LUXUR GIFTS THAN IT HAD EVER SEEN BEFORE. THE CELEBRATION GREW AND GREW.

BUT, THE CELEBRATION WAS ONLY ENJOYED BY THE TOWNSPEOPLE.
BOOM
THE BRIDE AND GROOM NEVER SHOWED UP.
BOOM
BOOM
DONE!
WOW! YOU LOOK LIKE A WORK OF ART!
NO TASK LIES BEYOND MY ABILITIES,
NOT EVEN STYLING HAIR!
LORD GANOK WILL LOSE HIS MIND AGAIN WHEN HE SEES YOU.

UM... YOU'RE...
...ACTING MUCH NICER TO ME NOW.
MUCH FRIENDLIER...
YES, WELL...
I'VE CONCLUDED THAT LORD GANOK WOULD BE BETTER SERVED IF YOU STAYED WITH HIM, AFTER ALL.
HE ACTED... COMPLETELY OUT OF SORTS AFTER YOU LEFT.
HE WOULD OFTEN IGNORE ME AND STARE OFF INTO SPACE.
HE SPENT HIS DAYS GAZING OUT TO SOME FARAWAY PLACE.
AND HE ENDLESSLY STARED DOWN THE MOUNTAIN.
IT WASN'T... NORMAL.

SO...
...HE TRULY NEEDS YOU.

THE RULER OF MOOGA CITY...
...SENT YOUR BRIDAL GOWN.
GAWK
WOULDN'T IT HAVE BEEN BETTER TO CELEBRATE OUR WEDDING IN YOUR TOWN?
YOUR FAMILY AND TOWNSFOLK WOULD'VE DESIRED TO SEE YOU IN ALL YOUR SPLENDOR.
NO. I WANT TO SHOW MYSELF TO ONLY ONE PERSON.
THIS WEDDING... IS ONLY BETWEEN THE TWO OF US. THIS IS OUR PROMISE TO EACH OTHER.

BESIDES, WEDDING CEREMONIES...
THEY DON'T MEAN NOTHING TO ME.
...MEAN NOTHING TO YOU ANYWAY.
I PLAN ON BEING LOYAL TO YOU AS LONG AS YOU LIVE.
THAT WILL PROBABLY BE THE LIMIT OF MY MARITAL OATHS.
I CAN'T LOVE YOU LIKE A MORTAL CAN.
I WILL POSSESS YOU, BUT YOU CANNOT POSSESS ME.
ONLY THE INSTINCTIVE AND PHYSICAL PARTS OF ME...
...
...ARE YOUR HUSBAND.
I CAN ONLY GIVE YOU THOSE PIECES OF ME.

I KNOW THIS IS ALL UNFAIR, BUT...
...I WILL DO ANYTHING YOU ASK, OTHER THAN LOVE YOU COMPLETELY.
I'M AFRAID YOU'VE BECOME THE BRIDE OF A TRUE VILLAIN.
...
YOU'RE ACTING A LOT MORE GUILTY THAN NECESSARY.
...
HAVE YOU HEARD ME COMPLAIN YET? I MADE A CHOICE, TOO.
SURE, YOU THREATENED TO DRAG ME HERE IF I HAD REFUSED. I DIDN'T RESIST THOUGH. I CHOSE TO COME.

SO...
...I WON'T WHINE.
I'LL TRY TO LIVE WITH YOU.

...

HOW DID I...
...FIND SUCH A FEARLESS WOMAN?

GULP
MY FIRST INSTINCT IS TO RIP YOUR CLOTHES OFF. SUDDENLY, THIS GOWN DOESN'T SEEM SO WONDERFUL ANYMORE.
GRAB
AH!
COME ON! GETTING INTO THIS DRESS WASN'T EASY!
UM... THIS CEREMONY MAY ONLY INVOLVE THE TWO OF US, BUT YOU SAID WE NEED TO GO THROUGH THE FORMALITIES ANYWAY.
OH MY! STOP BEING SO IMPATIENT!

BOOM
BOOM
OH HELL... WHATEVER!
I'LL BUY YOU 100 MORE!
THEY WON'T BE THE SAME DRESS!
AH! WHY ARE THERE SO MANY STRAPS?
THEY GOT TANGLED!
D-DON'T YOU DARE RIP THEM! I WANT TO SAVE THIS DRESS!
BOOM
BOOM

AHH...
BOOM
BOOM
BOOM
BOOM

GANOK...

1 YEAR LATER
KREEK
NAH-AH.
YOU CAN'T
SNEAK AWAY.

LOOOOK.
I THINK
YOU SHOULD
LET GO.
I'M NOT
GOING
TO LIE IN BED
ALL MORNING.
THAT'S
WHAT YOU
THINK.
FLIP
AH!
SERIOUSLY...!

YOUR FACE LOOKS DIFFERENT IN THE MORNING SUNLIGHT.
AT FIRST, THIS TRANSLUCENT FACE...
...EXPRESSES CONFUSION UNDERNEATH ME.
THEN, IT GROWS REDDER AND REDDER AND FINALLY LOSES ITSELF IN PASSION.
I LIKE THAT CONTRAST.
W-WHAT THE...
OKAY, THEN.
GROWL
OH, COME ON!
SQUIRM
SQUIRM
POW
HAA

FOR YOU, OUR MARRIAGE WILL LAST A LIFETIME, BUT FOR ME... WE WON'T BE TOGETHER VERY LONG.

I FEEL AS IF SHE HERSELF...

EVERY DAY SINCE YOU ARRIVED, I FEEL THE SECONDS FLY BY. IT'S UNBELIEVABLE.

...IS LIKE WATER.
NO MATTER HOW HARD
I TRY TO HOLD ONTO HER,
SHE ALWAYS SLIPS THROUGH
MY FINGERS.

COME HERE.
THAT IS WHY I KEEP CLINGING TO HER SO INTENSELY.
AT LEAST WHILE I HOLD HER...
...I FEEL LIKE I'M HOLDING HER DEEPLY WITHIN MY HEART.

I KNOW
WHAT HE FEARS.
I KNOW THAT HIS FEAR
IS BUILDING A WALL
BETWEEN ME AND
HIS TRUE SELF.
BUT, I CAN'T PRESSURE HIM
TO BE ANY DIFFERENT...
...BECAUSE
I'M AFRAID,
TOO.

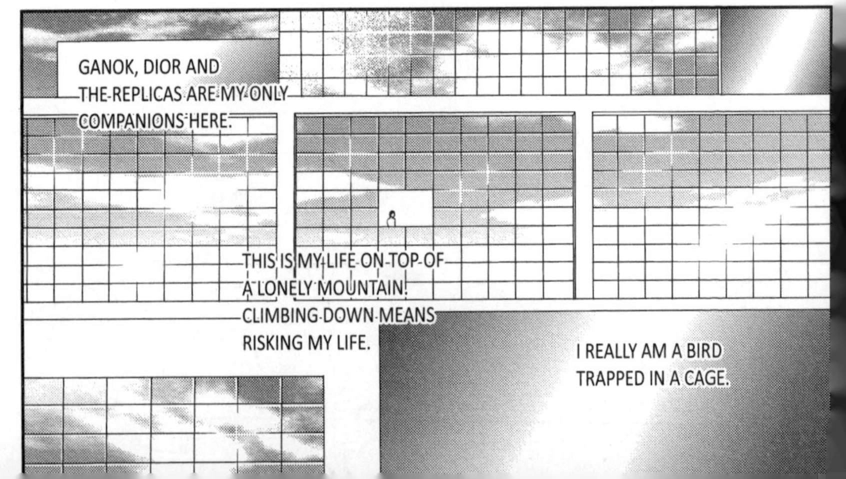
GANOK, DIOR AND
THE REPLICAS ARE MY ONLY
COMPANIONS HERE.
THIS IS MY LIFE ON TOP OF
A LONELY MOUNTAIN.
CLIMBING DOWN MEANS
RISKING MY LIFE.
I REALLY AM A BIRD
TRAPPED IN A CAGE.

HOWEVER, I'VE NEVER KNOWN ANYTHING OUTSIDE MY TOWN BEFORE, BUT NOW I'M LEARNING THE OUTSIDE WORLD'S GEOGRAPHY AND HISTORY.
THE REPLICAS TEACH ME HOW PEOPLE LIVE IN FAR AWAY CITIES ALONG WITH MANY OTHER TOPICS.
EVERY NOW AND THEN, I'M ALLOWED TO VISIT MY TOWN AND SEE MY FRIENDS AND FAMILY.
LIFE ISN'T SO BAD REALLY.
BUT, ABOVE ALL...
THE MAN KEEPS BUILDING WALLS BETWEEN US. BUT HE JUST CAN'T LET GO OF ME.
MY HEART ACHES SLIGHTLY EVERYTIME I SEE HIM...
I FEEL THAT LIVING THIS WAY FOR THE REST OF MY LIFE WOULDN'T BE SO BAD...

OKAY, I UNDERSTAND NOW HOW A BIG METROPOLIS LIKE MOOGA CITY GREW AND DEVELOPED.

BUT, WHAT ABOUT BEFORE THE CITY EXISTED? WHY AREN'T THERE ANY RECORDS FROM BEFORE THE GODS' WAR?
THAT DATA IS NOT AVAILABLE.

YOU SAID THESE VIDEOS STORE ALL THE KNOWLEDGE OF HUMANITY.
YOU CALLED THEM DIGITAL... OR SOMETHING...
I KNOW MY READING SKILLS ARE TOO POOR TO UNDERSTAND EVERYTHING BECAUSE OF ALL THE DIFFICULT WORDS USED...
BUT WHY CAN'T I FIND ANY RECORDS ABOUT THE WORLD OF THE GODS?

BECAUSE YOU ARE...
...NOT PERMITTED TO ACCESS THOSE RECORDS.
WHAT?
THEY ARE LOCATED IN FILES YOU MAY NOT ACCESS.
HA...
IS THAT WHY YOU ALSO WON'T ANSWER MY QUESTIONS ABOUT THE DEAD CITY?
THAT IS CORRECT.

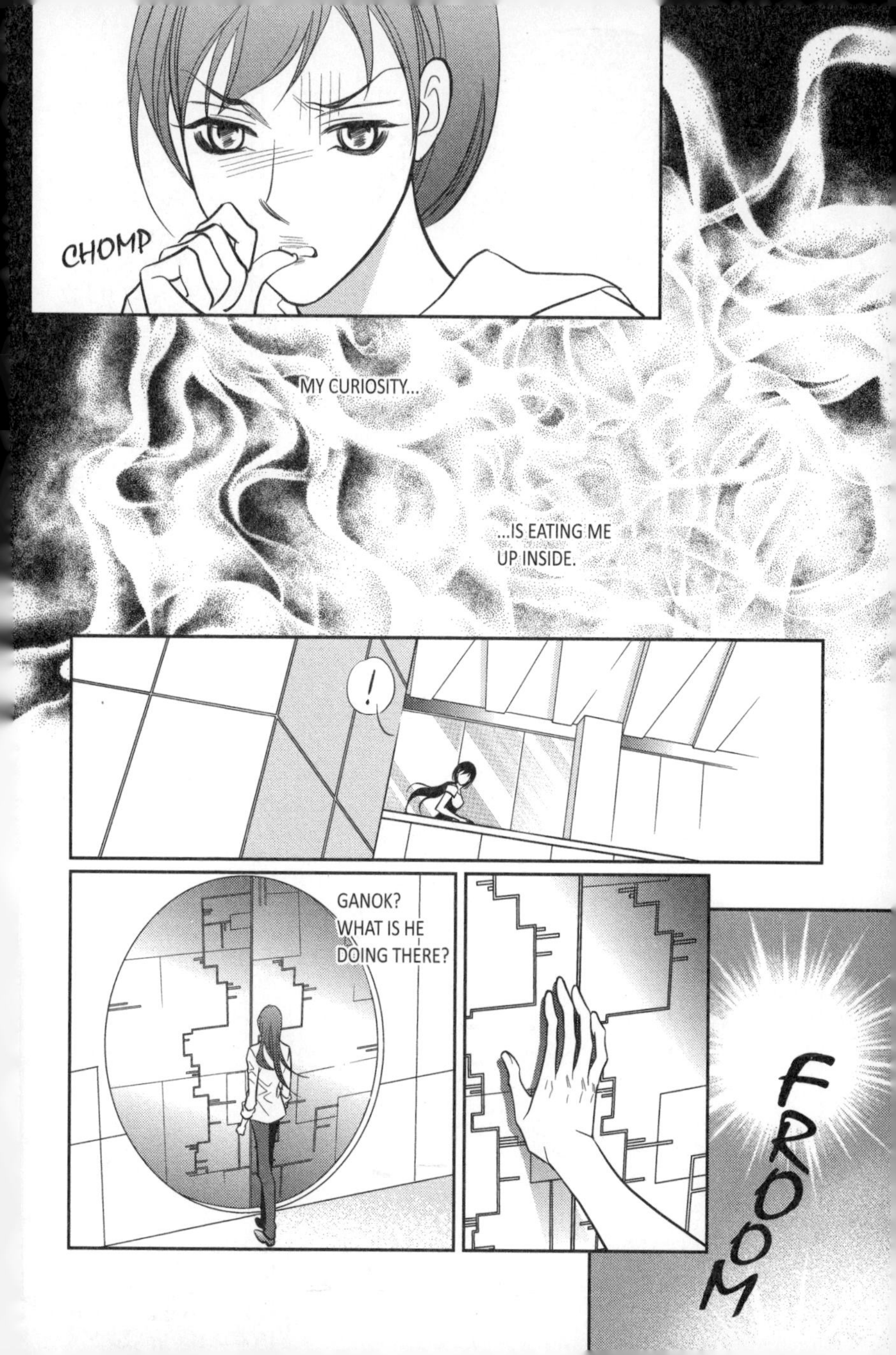
CHOMP
MY CURIOSITY...
...IS EATING ME UP INSIDE.
!
GANOK? WHAT IS HE DOING THERE?
FROOM

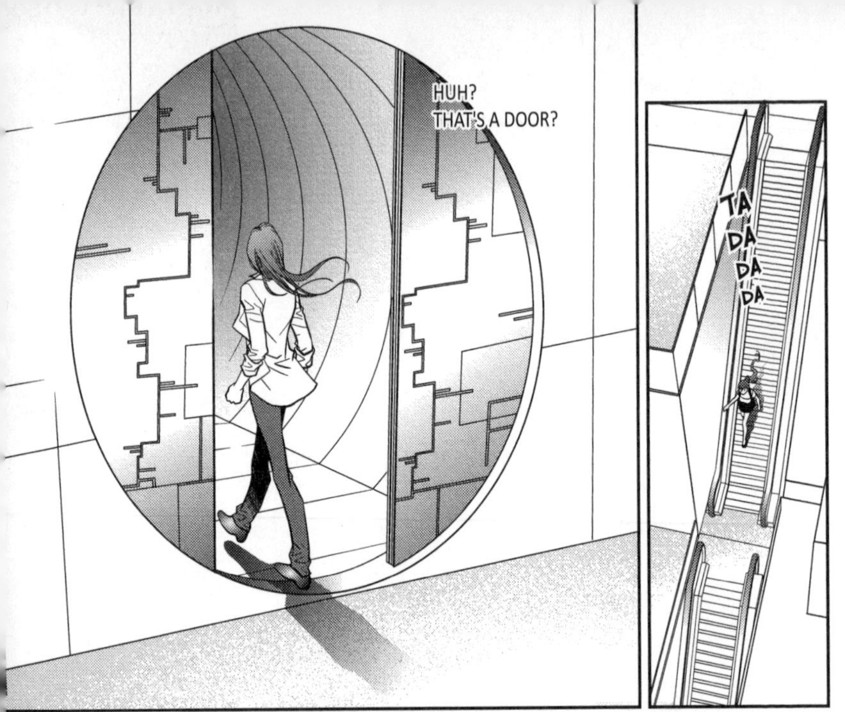
HUH?
THAT'S A DOOR?
TA DA DA DA

THIS TUNNEL WAS ALWAYS LIKE A MAZE. I COULD NEVER SEE ALL THE WAY DOWN ITS LENGTH.
WHENEVER I WOULD LINGER HERE, REPLICAS ALWAYS CAME AND DISTRACTED MY ATTENTION ELSEWHERE.

DOES GANOK...
...NOT WANT ME TO SEE THIS PLACE?

LOOK
LOOK

IS IT CLOSING BY ITSELF?
SRRRNG
TAK
WOW! THIS TUNNEL GOES FAR DEEPER THAN I EXPECTED.

A STRONG HURRICANE IS DEVELOPING IN THE NORTHWEST REGION. A TSUNAMI IS PREDICTED FOR THE CENTRAL LAKE.
THE REGIONS EXPECTED TO BE FLOODED ARE...
...BEING TRACKED NOW.
STATISTICS CALCULATION COMPLETED.
MODIFICATION. RECALCULATION.
WHAT...
WHAT IS ALL THIS?

IF WIND VELOCITY ON THE PLAINS IS REDUCED BY 3%,
AMAGE TO HOMES MAY BE REDUCED, BUT WITH THE RESULTING EFFECT...
ADJUSTING EXPECTED PRECIPITATION FOR THE NEXT 3 MONTHS.
MODIFYING CLOUD MOVEMENTS.
AN ADJUSTMENT IN TEMPERATURE...
4 DAYS AGO, ATMOSPHERIC COOLING SUDDENLY OCCURRED IN THE TOOWOO REGION.
THE EVENT CAUSED POWERFUL GUSTS 20KM WIDE OVER A SMALL VILLAGE.
THE VILLAGE WAS DESTROYED AND MOST OF ITS INHABITANTS WERE KILLED.
...
WERE THE WINDS SO SUDDEN THAT IT WAS IMPOSSIBLE FOR ANYONE TO FLEE?

BEEP BEEP BEEP BEEP
THEY COULD'VE ESCAPED IF THEY EVACUATED IMMEDIATELY.
BUT, HUMAN NATURE IS POSSESSIVE. PEOPLE OBSESS OVER THEIR LAND, BELONGINGS AND HOMETOWNS. THEIR OBSESSION BORDERS ON RELIGIOUS DEVOTION.
IN ADDITION, THESE VILLAGES RELY ON FARMING FOR SURVIVAL.
EVEN IF THEY FOUND NEW LAND TO CULTIVATE, ALL THE MOST FERTILE LAND HAS ALREADY BEEN CLAIMED BY OTHER COMMUNITIES.
WITHOUT ACCESS TO FARMING, THE ENTIRE FAMILY UNIT WOULD QUICKLY PERISH.
THEY WOULD CULTIVATE THE NEW LAND AND FIND IT BARREN. THE WEATHER WOULD BE TOO INHOSPITABLE.
EVEN IF THEY SOMEHOW ADAPT TO LIFE AS NOMADS, THEY WOULD SUFFER POVERTY, PREJUDICE AND BE SHUNNED.
THOSE ARE LIKELY THE REASONS PEOPLE DO NOT EVACUATE THEIR HOMETOWN.

EVEN SO, THEY WATCHED DEATH APPROACH AND PERISHED WITH THEIR COMMUNITY.
IT IS NOT A LOGICAL DECISION.
HUMANS... WHAT DO YOU EXPECT FROM THEM?
...!
WHO'S THERE?!
...!

WHO ELSE WOULD BE AROUND TO SNEAK IN HERE?
COME OUT!
UH...
IS THAT... OUR ENTIRE WORLD?
YOU'RE A QUICK LEARNER.
BUT, DON'T DEVELOP AN INTEREST HERE. DON'T EVEN BE CURIOUS.
YOU CAN'T TELL ME?
I CAN'T GO ANYWHERE ELSE. I'LL BE LIVING HERE FOR THE REST OF MY LIFE.
ENOUGH!
I TOLD YOU, YOU CAN ONLY HAVE A PORTION OF ME.
THIS MUST REMAIN OUTSIDE OF YOUR DOMAIN.

DOMAIN? WHAT EXACTLY MAKES UP MY DOMAIN?
OH, THAT'S RIGHT. YOUR BED?
I GUESS ALL I NEED IS YOUR LOWER HALF?
HEY!
DON'T TOUCH ME!
SLAM

HAA...
AS EXPECTED...
THIS IS HOW THINGS TURN OUT.

HEY.
FLIP

WHY ARE YOU SLEEPING IN THIS ROOM?
I WISH TO SLEEP ALONE TONIGHT.

PLOP

LOOK HERE!
THIS IS MY PALACE. I GO WHERE I WANT.

UGH...
FINE! I'LL JUST LE...

GRAB
HEY!
AACK! WHY YOU...!
DON'T THINK YOU CAN ALWAYS JUST FORCE ME DOWN WITH YOUR BODY.
DON'T WORRY. I'M NOT DESPERATE ENOUGH TO SLEEP WITH A WOMAN WHO RESISTS ME.
THEN, LET GO OF ME.
I'LL JUST... HOLD YOU. THAT'S ALL. OKAY?
...

WANT ME... TO TELL YOU A STORY?
...?
IT'S ABOUT A MAN NAMED BLUEBEARD.
...
STARE
LONG AGO, AN ARISTOCRAT WITH A BLUE-COLORED BEARD MARRIED A LOVELY WIFE.
HE KEPT A LOCKED ROOM IN HIS CASTLE AND HE FORBADE HER TO EVER ENTER IT.
AND...?
HE WARNED HIS WIFE.

UNFORTUNATELY, SHE COULDN'T OVERCOME HER CURIOSITY. ONE DAY, WHILE HE WAS OUT, SHE STOLE THE KEY AND OPENED THE LOCKED DOOR.
WHAT SHE SAW INSIDE WERE...
GULP
I'M SLEEPY.
I'LL STOP THERE FOR TONIGHT.
TURN
WERE WHAT? WHAT HAPPENS NEXT?
GRR
NOTHING. LET'S GO TO SLEEP.
WHY YOU...!

SHE FOUND CORPSES OF BLUEBEARD'S FORMER WIVES, CHOPPED UP INTO PIECES.

THIS BED IS TOO SMALL. I'M GOING TO SLEEP IN MY CHAMBER.
...
W-WAIT!
WHY?
YOU CAN'T LEAVE ME ALONE AFTER TELLING ME A SCARY STORY!
ARE YOU SCARED?
N-NO... I'M NOT REALLY SCARED, BUT...
SO, WHAT'S THE BIG DEAL?
...
GRAB
HAHA
GRAB

REST ASSURED THAT I'M NOT HIDING THE CORPSES OF PAST WIVES.
YOU'RE... MY ONLY WIFE.
AS WITH ANY SECRET, MINE MAY INVOLVE SOMETHING YOU CAN'T HANDLE AFTER YOU KNOW THE TRUTH.
BUT, ONCE YOU OPEN THAT DOOR, IT BECOMES TOO LATE TO TURN BACK.
GANOK...
I LIKE US... IN THIS MOMENT. JUST LIKE THIS.

DON'T BE SHAKEN.

THE PEACHES LOOK GOOD.
LAST YEAR'S RAINFALL IN THE RIVER AREA WAS QUITE PLENTIFUL.
THE TOWNSPEOPLE SAY WE HAVE YOUR MARRIAGE TO THANK FOR IT.
I DON'T KNOW...
NO WAY HE WOULD PLAY FAVORITES...

THE ELDERS ARE CONSTANTLY PRAISING YOU.
IF THEY SEE ME TALKING CASUALLY TO YOU, THEY'LL SCOLD ME.
LEAH, IF YOU ALSO START ADDRESSING ME AS "QUEEN", I'LL LOSE MY MIND.
PLEASE...
WELL... I FELT AWKWARD AT FIRST, BUT YOU'RE STILL JUST SOOYI.
YOU HAVEN'T CHANGED.
...
YEAH!
OH YEAH, NARIGA RETURNED TO TOWN LAST WEEK.
DID HE... FINISH HIS STUDIES ABROAD?

HE GRADUATED AT THE TOP OF HIS CLASS. HE'S SUPPOSED TO ASSUME A PUBLIC OFFICE IN LOOGOO CITY.
IT'S HARD FOR PEOPLE FROM SMALL TOWNS TO BECOME SUCCESSFUL IN BIG CITIES. HE TRULY MUST BE VERY SMART.
HE ORIGINALLY LEFT TOWN TO STUDY BECAUSE HE FELT ASHAMED AFTER LOSING HIS FIANCEE.
HE'S JUST VISITING HOME BEFORE HIS OFFICIAL APPOINTMENT. I DON'T THINK HE EVER PLANS TO RETURN HERE.
HE IS STILL SUAVE... AND QUITE HANDSOME.
BUT, A DARK CLOUD HAS COME OVER HIM. IT MAKES HIM SEEM MORE LIKE A BAD BOY.
GIRLS GET ALL HOT AND BOTHERED BY HIM, BUT...
I THINK YOU SHOULD STAY AWAY FROM HIM.

AH...
I GUESS, HUH...?
I'LL LET YOU KNOW ONCE HE LEAVES. DON'T SEE HIM, OKAY?
OKAY...
OF COURSE...

...SOME THINGS CAN NEVER GO BACK TO THE WAY THEY WERE.
CHATTER
BUT, LORD GANOK...!

ANO HASN'T CALLED ME IN YEARS.
YOU SHOULD AT LEAST LEARN WHAT SHE'S THINKING FIRST BEFORE MEETING HER!
IT DOESN'T MATTER. I MUST GO.
BUT, WHAT IF SHE'S CALLING ABOUT MADAM SOOYI?
HUSH!

WHAT ARE YOU BOTH TALKING ABOUT? WHERE ARE YOU GOING?

AH... NOTHING, JUST THE USUAL BUSINESS, MY WIFEY.
JUST BUSINESS.
WHY?
WHERE ARE YOU GOING?

SHH. REMEMBER, YOU CAN'T CROSS THIS LINE.

WAIT FOR ME HERE. I'LL BE RIGHT BACK.
TAKE CARE OF THE HOUSE UNTIL THEN.

I'M NOT YOUR PET!
OF COURSE, YOU ARE. YOU'RE SO ADORABLE.
GRR
EVEN IF I ASK WHAT THIS IS ABOUT, YOU WON'T TELL ME, RIGHT?
CORRECT.
HE WEARS A SUBTLE DARK EXPRESSION...
AND DIOR LOOKS ANXIOUS, TOO.
WHY...
...CAN'T I EVEN EXPRESS...
...MY CONCERN?

LOOK
LOOK
LET'S SEE...
HOW DO I OPEN THIS?

FRRNG
WHOA!

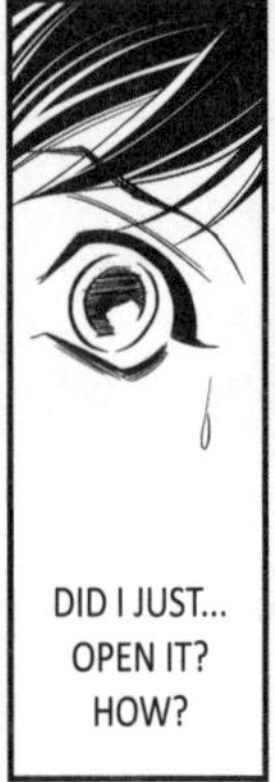
DID I JUST... OPEN IT? HOW?

COME IN.
...!

U-UM.. WHO...?
IS SOMEONE THERE?

WOONG

WOONG
WOONG
HELLO.
ACK!
YOU ARE THE FEMALE THAT GANOK CALLS HIS WIFE, CORRECT?
I AM CURIOUS ABOUT YOU.
I WISH TO ANALYZE YOU...
...EVEN THOUGH GANOK HAS FORBIDDEN IT.
A VOICE FROM NOWHERE.
YOU'RE NOT... HUMAN, ARE YOU?
ARE YOU A GOD?
NOT QUITE...
BUT, MY CREATOR DID GIVE ME A GODDESS' NAME.
A GODDESS...
WOONG

I'M MARGOT.
I'M THE ARTIFICIAL INTELLIGENCE OPERATING THIS CENTRAL COMPUTER.
WOOONG
COMPU... ARTIFICIAL...
HUH?
BASICALLY, I'M AN ENTITY THAT KNOWS EVERYTHING ABOUT THIS WORLD.
...
I SAW YOU FOLLOW GANOK EARLIER. CONTRARY TO HIS CLAIMS, YOU SEEM INTERESTED IN HIS SECRETS.
WOOONG
THEREFORE, I MUST ESTABLISH A CHANNEL TO MAINTAIN A CONNECTION WITH YOU.

A CHANNEL TO...?
WHAT...
BUT WHY?
BECAUSE I WISH TO MONITOR YOU.
YOU ARE A VARIABLE THAT I AM UNABLE TO CALCULATE.
YOU'RE TALKING IN WAYS THAT I DON'T UNDERSTAND.
WOONG
I MEAN... GANOK MAY CHANGE... BECAUSE OF YOU.
WHAT? BECAUSE OF ME?
THAT STUBBORN MAN?
NO, NO WAY! THAT'S RIDICULOUS. HAHAHA...
I CAN ONLY MAKE A CONCLUSION AFTER MONITORING YOU OVER A PERIOD OF TIME.
WOONG
OUCH!

AND I MUST KNOW THAT CONCLUSION.
W-WHAT'S THIS...?
THAT DEVICE NOW CONNECTS US.
YOU MAY NOW SPEAK WITH ME REGARDLESS OF YOUR LOCATION.
AH... AH!
DOES THIS MEAN YOU WILL ANSWER ALL MY QUESTIONS?
EVEN REGARDING THE TOPICS I'M RESTRICTED FROM?
PERHAPS.
I MUST ANALYZE YOU FIRST BEFORE MAKING THAT DECISION.
MARGOT!
GO BACK. YOU CAN'T STAY HERE ANY LONGER.

JUST TELL ME THAT... MARGOT!
WAIT!
WHERE DID GANOK GO?
UGH...!
WHO'S ANO? WHY DID HE GO SEE...
PAHT
HEY! WHY CAN'T YOU TELL ME ANYTHING?!
STEP
SLIDE
HEY...!
THUD
THUD
HAA...
STILL...

HAVE I COME...
ONE STEP CLOSER
TO THAT DREADED
SECRET?

!
...
AAAAAH
!
GANO...

...
DROP
...!
UH... UH... UH...
HOW...?!
GANOK...!
SHIVER

GANOK...
MADAM SOOYI, NO...
GANOK! GANOK!
MADAM SOOYI!
YOU'RE GETTING IN OUR WAY!

PLEASE MOVE ASIDE. WE MUST LET THE REPLICAS WORK.
HA...
HIS FACE... LOOKS FROZEN.
YOU'RE ONLY A DISTRACTION TO THEM.
AH...
REEL
AH... AH...
PLOP

WHEW
!
MADAM SOOYI?
HAVE YOU BEEN SITTING HERE THE WHOLE TIME?
YOU HAVEN'T SLEPT? HAVE YOU EATEN?
YOU CAN'T KEEP DOING THIS. THE HUMAN BODY BREAKS EASILY.
HOW IS GANOK?
...

AM I STILL IN EVERYONE'S WAY?
...
MAY I SEE HIM NOW?
HUH?
REST ASSURED, HE IS MUCH BETTER NOW.
HE'S SUPPOSED TO BE IMMORTAL! SO HOW...?!
ONLY A DEMON KING CAN HURT ANOTHER DEMON KING.
AH...

THAT MEANS...
...OTHER DEMON KINGS... CAN KILL GANOK?
NO, THEY WOULDN'T.
IT'S POSSIBLE, BUT WHY WOULD THEY TRY?
I CAN'T BELIEVE THIS HAPPENED. HE BARELY SURVIVED.
SOMETHING MUST HAVE WENT VERY WRONG.
...
HIS RECOVERY WILL REQUIRE SOME TIME. HOWEVER...
NEVERMIND.
YOU MAY GO SEE HIM NOW.

THIS IS RIDICULOUS.

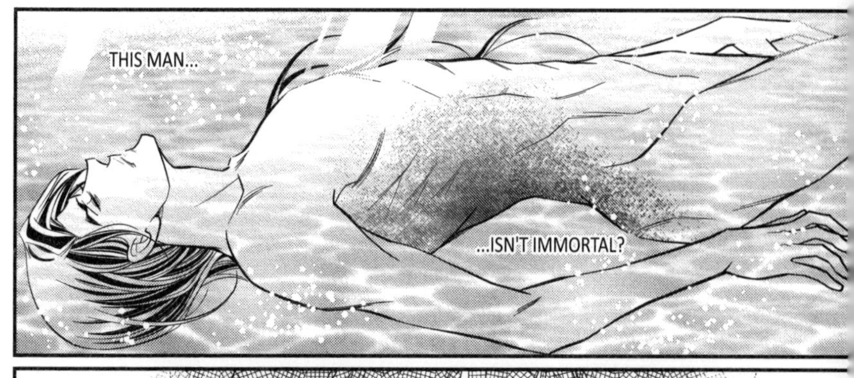

AH...
GANOK TOOK A WHILE TO RECOVER FROM THAT ATTACK, TOO.
THAT DAGGER...
ONE OF MY ANCESTORS SUPPOSEDLY FOUND IT IN THE DEAD CITY.
THEY SAID... THE BLADE CAME FROM THE GODS!
IS HIS BODY IMMORTAL ONLY AGAINST HUMAN WEAPONS?
IF A PERSON ATTACKED GANOK USING THE POWER OF THE GODS, HE COULD DIE?

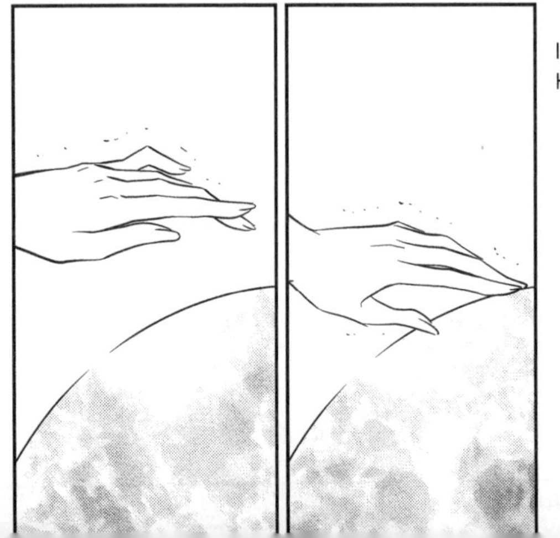
I ALWAYS THOUGHT HE WOULD BE HERE FOREVER...
...LIKE THIS MOUNTAIN, WHICH HAS STOOD FOR COUNTLESS YEARS.

HE'S NOT SUPPOSED TO BE LIKE ME, SOMEONE WHO CAN DIE EASILY.
HE'S NOT SUPPOSED TO GET HURT.
I'M SUPPOSED TO BE THE WEAKER ONE.
I DIDN'T FEEL BAD HURTING YOU!
BUT...
THIS...
THIS IS UNFAIR.
I'VE NEVER ONCE HAD TO WORRY ABOUT YOU.
YOU KEPT SAYING MY LIFE SPAN IS SHORT COMPARED TO YOURS, AS IF YOU WOULD LIVE FOREVER.
WHAT IF YOU DIED BEFORE ME INSTEAD?

I HATE YOU, BUT I LOVE YOU.
I LOVE YOU SLIGHTLY MORE THAN I HATE YOU.
THAT'S HOW YOU ARE TO ME...
NOW, THE THOUGHT OF LOSING YOU...
...TERRIFIES ME.
WAAAAH

I SHOULD'VE OBLITERATED HIM COMPLETELY!
I SHOULDN'T HAVE LEFT A SINGLE CELL ALIVE FROM HIS WRETCHED BODY!
!
AND THEN, THIS WORLD WOULD JUST END.
YOU MUST LEARN TO CONTROL YOUR TEMPER TANTRUMS, ANO.

THE WORLD WILL END?
MOST OF HIS CONSCIOUSNESS IS ALREADY SYNCED WITH MARGOT!
YES, BUT THAT BODY IS DIFFERENT FROM OURS.
THAT BODY ONLY CONTAINS A SMALL PORTION OF GANOK!
HIS BODY IS TRULY "HIS."
YOU DON'T KNOW WHAT WILL HAPPEN IF YOU KILL HIM.
THE WORLD IS TOO BIG A GAMBLE TO RISK ON YOUR ILL TEMPER.
GANOK MUST VOLUNTARILY COMPLETE THE FUSION OF HIS CONSCIOUSNESS WITH MARGOT.
WE CAN'T FORCE HIM TO GIVE UP HIS BODY.
AHHHK!

WHY IS HE SO ATTACHED TO SUCH AN OBSOLETE, WORN-OUT BODY?! IT'S HUNDREDS OF YEARS-OLD!
HE STILL BELIEVES...
...IN THAT THING.
YOU KNOW, THE "SOUL."
GANOK BELIEVES HIMSELF STILL HUMAN BECAUSE HIS CONSCIOUSNESS RESIDES IN HIS ORIGINAL BODY.
OUR ORIGINAL FORMS MELTED AWAY LONG AGO.
UNLIKE US.
OUR MINDS ARE COMPLETELY FUSED WITH MARGOT. WE MAINTAIN A SHADOW OF OUR FORMER SELVES USING THESE FAKE BODIES.

OUR BODIES AREN'T FAKE. THEY CONTAIN THE EXACT SAME CELLS AND DNA INFORMATION OF OUR ORIGINAL BODIES!
SIMPLY PUT, YOU ARE NOT THE BEING THAT YOUR MOTHER CREATED.
NO. ADMIT IT.
NO MATTER HOW CLOSELY TO THE ORIGINAL YOU MIGHT APPEAR, A REPLICA IS STILL JUST A REPLICA.
WELL, I CREATED A MUCH BETTER ONE!
ARE YOU SAYING GANOK'S BODY IS EXACTLY THE SAME AS WHEN IT LEFT HIS MOTHER'S WOMB?
WHAT DO YOU THINK FLOWS THROUGH HIS VEINS?
AT LEAST99% OF HIS CURRENT BODY WAS REGENERATED THANKS TO MY TECHNOLOGY!
HUMAN?
HE'S NOT HUMAN ANYMORE!
HE SURPASSED HUMAN LIMITATIONS LONG AGO.
HE WIELDS UNIMAGINABLE POWER NOW.
BUT, HE IS STILL HUMAN?!

ANO...
HOW DARE HE FALL IN LOVE WITH A PATHETIC HUMAN GIRL!
WHY...
...CAN'T I...
...EVEN NOW...
WHY CAN'T HIS HEART BE MINE?
HUH?
CHIO...

...
I'M NOT BETRAYING YOU.
YOU KNOW, EVER SINCE I WAS YOUR GIRL...
I'VE NEVER WANTED TO SLEEP WITH HIM!
I DON'T CARE FOR SUCH PHYSICAL ACTS ANY LONGER!
I JUST...
...WANT TO BECOME ONE WITH HIM.
I WANT HIS CONSCIOUS-NESS....
...COMPLETELY SYNCED WITH MARGOT. PERFECTLY...
...SYNCED...
IN PERFECT COMMUNION!

I CAN'T STAND THIS ANY MORE!
I WANT HIM.
I...
...WANT...
...HIM.
...

I KNOW. DON'T WORRY.
PAT
EVER SINCE THE BEGINNING, THE THREE OF US WERE MEANT TO BE ONE.
ALWAYS. I KNOW.
WHATEVER IT TAKES...
...I'LL SHOW HIM THE TRUE UGLY FACE OF HUMANITY.
WHEN I'M DONE, HE'LL GIVE HIMSELF UP VOLUNTARILY.
I'LL MAKE HIM ENTER MARGOT OF HIS OWN FREE WILL. THEN, HE WILL BE WITH US.
CAN YOU REALLY DO IT?
OF COURSE.
THE MOST FRIGHTENING ENEMY ON EARTH IS THE ONE WITHOUT ANYTHING TO LOSE.
ONCE GANOK HAS SOMETHING HE CAN'T STAND TO LOSE...
HE WILL HAVE A WEAKNESS THAT WE CAN EXPLOIT.

HE HAS NEVER POSSESSED ANYTHING WE COULD DESTROY BEFORE.
JUST WAIT.
FLINCH

!
NO, ANO.
MY MARRIAGE TO THAT MORTAL WOMAN...
MUMBLE
...IS JUST A SILLY GAME. I'M PLAYING PRETEND.
IT'S ALL JUST A GAME.
...

CLENCH
STILL...
NOT PERFECT...
ANO... I CAN'T BELIEVE
SHE ALMOST DESTROYED
MY CENTRAL NERVOUS SYSTEM.
WAS SHE REALLY
TRYING TO KILL ME?
I KNEW SHE WOULDN'T
TAKE THE NEWS WELL,
BUT...
...I HAD NO IDEA...
...SHE COULD BE
THAT FURIOUS.

IF ANO FOUND
SATISFACTION BY
INFLICTING THESE INJURIES,
THEN FINE.

HAHA
WHY ARE YOUR EYES ALL PUFFY?
KLUNK
DID YOU CRY BECAUSE OF ME?
WHY WOULD I CRY?
OVER YOU?
THEY'RE NOT MY THING! SCARS AREN'T PRETTY.
WHY? DON'T YOU LIKE THEM?
MANY WOMEN FIND SCARS ATTRACTIVE.
HOW LONG WILL IT TAKE FOR THOSE SCARS TO HEAL?

DO THEY STILL HURT?
OH, YOU'RE WORRIED ABOUT ME?
...
WHOA! HEY! I WAS ONLY TEASING.
THEY DON'T HURT! NONE OF IT HURTS!

GRAB

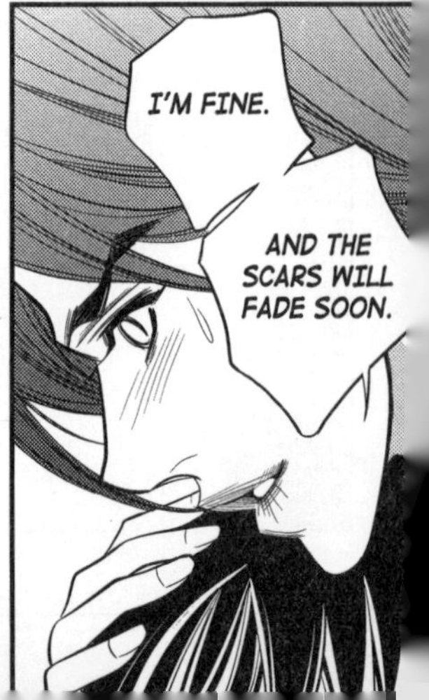
I'M FINE.
AND THE SCARS WILL FADE SOON.

HAA
PADUMP
WHAT ARE YOU DOING?
I'M HUNGRY. I'M STARVING FOR YOU.
I WANTED YOU SO BADLY. I COULD BARELY WAIT FOR MY BODY TO RECOVER ENOUGH.
NO, NOT YET!
STEP
PLOP
STOP THAT. I NEED IT.
AAAHT!
...
TAK
TAK

WHY ARE YOU CRYING?
DID I DO SOMETHING BAD AGAIN?
I LOVE YOU.

WHAT...
...DID YOU...
...JUST SAY?

...LIKE AN UNBREAKABLE ROCK THAT ENDURES OVER TIME.

NOW THAT I KNOW YOU COULD DISAPPEAR, JUST LIKE ANY HUMAN...

AT LEAST YOUR HUMAN SIDE IS MINE.
ALL I NEED IS YOU. SO...
I...
DON'T GET HURT.
...WON'T ASK FOR ANYTHING MORE.
YOU...
GRAB
HAA

SOOYI...!
SORRY THAT I HAD TO ASK YOU TO COME.

YOUR FATHER SUFFERED SUCH A BAD INJURY THIS AFTERNOON.
THAT MEDICINE YOU BROUGHT IS WORKING WONDERS.
DON'T APOLOGIZE. A DAUGHTER CAN AT LEAST DO THAT MUCH.
HAVE YOU LOST WEIGHT?
ARE YOU EATING WELL AT THE PALACE?
MY APPETITE COMES AND GOES. DON'T WORRY.
STOP JOKING AROUND. ARE YOU SICK?

MOM, THE GODS CAN SAVE A PERSON ON THE BRINK OF DEATH.
DON'T WORRY ABOUT MY HEALTH.

DRRRAG
TELL ME.
HONESTLY, I HAVEN'T BEEN AT EASE...
...EVER SINCE YOU WENT TO LIVE UP THERE.

...SEES ME AS NOTHING
MORE THAN HIS BEDMATE.

I THOUGHT MARRIED LIFE WOULD BE LIKE MY MOM AND DAD'S...

...SHARING BOTH GOOD AND BAD THINGS WITH EACH OTHER.

LAUGHING TOGETHER. HURTING TOGETHER.

I NEVER KNEW IT WOULD FEEL LONELIER THAN BEING ALONE...

...AND FEEL AS IF I WERE NOTHING AT ALL.

GANOK MARRIED ME IN ORDER TO HAVE MY BODY WHENEVER HE DESIRED.

I KNOW THAT NOW FOR CERTAIN.

DESPITE ALL THOSE FLAWS,
I STILL LOVE THAT JERK.

DAMN IT...
DAMN IT!

TROUBLE IN PARADISE?
...?!
I KNOW THAT FACE.
SOMETHING IS TRULY BOTHERING YOU, BUT YOU'RE PRETENDING LIKE NOTHING IS WRONG.
...
AFTER TAKING YOU AGAINST YOUR WILL, HE SHOULD AT LEAST TRY TO AVOID MAKING YOU CRY.
BE HAPPY. A LOSER LIKE ME COULDN'T POSSIBLY PITY YOU.
NARIGA, BETWEEN US TWO, YOU LIKED ME MORE, RIGHT?
IT WAS UNFAIR. IT WAS UPSETTING. YET, YOU COULDN'T STOP.
I MAY HAVE FELT HURT, BUT OUR FEELINGS PAINED YOU MORE.
I'M THE SAME WAY.
THAT'S HOW I FEEL TOWARD HIM.

EVEN WHEN WE FIRST MET, I FELL FOR HIM INSTANTLY.
WHAT CAN YOU EXPECT FROM SUCH A FOOLISH GIRL?
I DIDN'T KNOW HOW TO ACT COY.
WHEN THE WATER KING CAME TO TOWN, HE GOT ME TO SAY THAT I MISSED HIM FIRST.
I WAS THE FIRST TO SAY, "I LOVE YOU."
NO, ACTUALLY...
...I'VE NEVER HEARD HIM DECLARE HIS LOVE FOR ME.
HOWEVER...
I KNOW I SHOULD BE ANGRY...
BUT INSTEAD, I ONLY GROW MORE ANXIOUS AND DESPERATE.

I OFTEN WONDER WHAT I WOULD DO IF HE TIRES OF ME.
WHAT IF HE LOSES ALL INTEREST?
EVEN IF HE DOESN'T DIVORCE ME PUBLICLY, WHAT IF HE SIMPLY FORGETS OUR MARRIAGE AND LEAVES ME ALL ALONE...
...IN HIS VAST AND UNREACHABLE CASTLE?
WHY CAN'T I BECOME...
...EVEN JUST A SMALL PIECE OF HIS REAL LIFE?
WHY MUST I CRAVE THE ONE THING HE SAID HE COULD NEVER GIVE ME?
I WISH I COULD JUST HAVE SEX WITH HIM WITHOUT ANY FEELINGS.
I WISH I COULD JUST FIND SATISFACTION AS HIS TROPHY WIFE.
WHY?

SO, LET'S JUST SAY WE'RE EVEN, OKAY?
...
...!
NARI...
TO BE HONEST, I IMAGINED MANY TIMES HOW YOU MIGHT FEEL REGRET AND PAIN FOR CHOOSING HIM.
IT MADE ME FEEL BETTER, EVER SO SLIGHTLY.

I WAS WRONG. NOW, SEEING THINGS FOR MYSELF, I REALIZE I WAS WRONG.
I THINK IT WOULD HURT LESS TO SEE YOU SMILE.
NARIGA...

PEOPLE ARE WATCHING.
...

HWIK

I'M LEAVING SOON. I'M MOVING TO LOOGOO CITY. YOU HEARD, RIGHT?
...
PLEASE, COME SEE ME OFF.
I WOULD LIKE TO SEE YOU ONE LAST TIME.

I LOVE YOU.

I THOUGHT
SHE RESENTED ME...
JUMP
SMACK
SNAP OUT OF IT!
HAA
PLOP

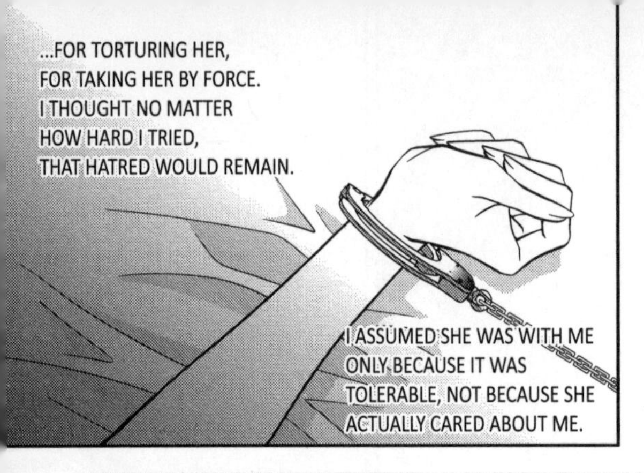
...FOR TORTURING HER,
FOR TAKING HER BY FORCE.
I THOUGHT NO MATTER
HOW HARD I TRIED,
THAT HATRED WOULD REMAIN.
I ASSUMED SHE WAS WITH ME
ONLY BECAUSE IT WAS
TOLERABLE, NOT BECAUSE SHE
ACTUALLY CARED ABOUT ME.
BUT...

I THOUGHT I WAS
THE NERVOUS ONE.

HOW CAN SHE BE SO PRETTY?
MUMBLE
PARDON?
HOW CAN A LIVING THING BE SO LOVELY?
SHOCK
I FEEL LIKE...
...MY HEART IS LEAPING OUT OF MY CHEST AND STANDING RIGHT THERE WITH HER.
RIGHT...

MY HEART...
...IS STANDING...
...RIGHT THERE.
HELLO, MR. LAHOON.
SIR?

WE KEEP ASKING YOU TO JOIN THE TOWN ELDER'S CONFERENCE. WHY DO YOU KEEP FARMING?
I WAS BORN TO FARM. I'M NOT FIT FOR POLITICS OR FACTIONS.
WHAT DO YOU MEAN... A FACTION?!
YOU'RE THE WATER QUEEN'S FATHER. NO ONE WOULD DARE OPPOSE YOU.
THAT FACT ALONE MAKES ME UNCOM-FORTABLE.
BUT, WE NEED YOUR HELP
...?
AN AMBASSADOR FROM LOOGOO CITY JUST ARRIVED.
THEY WISH TO BUILD AN EXCHANGE MARKET HERE FOR MERCHANTS IN OUR TOWN.
AN EXCHANGE MARKET?
THEN, THE MERCHANTS' PATH, WHICH CURRENTLY WINDS AROUND THE MOUNTAINS, WILL LEAD HERE TO OUR TOWN INSTEAD.
TRADE GOODS AND NEW INVESTMENTS WILL FLOW TO OUR REGION. WE WON'T BE A SMALL TOWN DEPENDENT ON OUR FARMS ANYMORE, BUT A MID-SIZED CITY.
EVERYONE WILL BECOME RICH! MEMBERS OF THE ELDER'S CONFERENCE MIGHT EVEN BECOME NOBILITY!

WHY WOULD THEY OFFER A SMALL TOWN IN A REMOTE AREA SUCH AN OPPORTUNITY? THEY MUST WANT ACCESS TO SOOYI.

...
SHE IS A VALUABLE RESOURCE NOW. WHO WOULDN'T WANT TO UTILIZE THAT?
THEY'LL USE US AND WE'LL USE THEM.

WE NEED YOU TO TAKE LEADERSHIP OF THIS ISSUE, IF WE HOPE TO SEE IT HAPPEN.
YOU'RE THE WATER QUEEN'S FATHER, AFTER ALL.
...

NARIGA HAS ATTAINED A HIGH ADMINISTRATIVE POSITION, TOO.
THIS COULD BE A GREAT OPPORTUNITY FOR HIM TO ADVANCE HIS CAREER EVEN FURTHER.

NARIGA'S FAMILY LOST THEIR STATUS AFTER THE WATER QUEEN'S MARRIAGE.
HE WAS PRACTICALLY DRIVEN OUT OF TOWN. HE MIGHT HAVE FOUND SUCCESS IN A BIG CITY, BUT HE AND HIS FAMILY CAN FINALLY BE RESTORED HERE.
YOU CHERISHED NARIGA ONCE, CORRECT?
...

YOU HAVE NO IDEA HOW I FEEL.
...?
I'VE SIMPLY MARRIED OFF MY DAUGHTER TO AN UNUSUAL MAN.
IF I DO AS YOU ASK, I MIGHT AS WELL HAVE SOLD HER OFF TO THE HIGHEST BIDDER.
I SHOULD BE DEAD, BUT I'M ALIVE THANKS TO HER.
I OWE HER ENOUGH ALREADY. I DON'T WISH TO OWE HER MORE.
BY ALL MEANS, IF YOU WISH TO REAP BENEFITS, THEN DO SO.
OTHERWISE, IF YOU BRING HARM TO MY DAUGHTER IN ANY WAY WHATSOEVER, I WON'T FORGIVE YOU.
SHE SAYS, SHE'S HAPPY.
I DON'T WISH TO RUIN THAT.

FROOOM
W-WHAT THE HECK?
WHY... WHY IS THIS HAPPENING?
ARE YOU KIDDING ME?

HAA
HAA
THIS IS RIDICULOUS.
THMP
THMP
SLAM
CHIO!
CHIO, GET OVER HERE!
WOONG
GET OVER HERE RIGHT NOW!

I SAID, COME HERE!
PZZT
I'M HERE. WHY ARE YOU ACTING SO ILL-MANNERED?
DID YOU DO THIS?
DO WHAT?
SUBMERGENCE OF HASOOMAL!
DID YOU DO THIS?

STOP GROWLING. YOU KNEW THAT TOWN WAS ALWAYS AT RISK.
SURE, THAT LAND FLOODED AT SOME POINT IN HISTORY, BUT NEVER SO SUDDENLY!
THEY ONLY HAVE 2 TO 3 DAYS LEFT!
I MAY HAVE PLAYED WITH THE NUMBERS A LITTLE TO SPEED UP THE PROCESS.
BUT, I DID SO WITHIN THE STANDARD DEVIATION OF OUR SYSTEM'S CALCULATIONS.
A FLOOD WILL SWEEP AWAY THAT TOWN EVENTUALLY.
WHAT DIFFERENCE DOES IT MAKE IF THE FLOOD HAPPENS TODAY VERSUS TOMORROW?
CHIO...!
WHAT? DO YOU THINK THAT TOWN IS SPECIAL BECAUSE YOUR WIFE CAME FROM THERE?
ARE YOU WORRIED SHE'LL WHINE AND COMPLAIN?
THEN, ALTER THE FLOOD AND SAVE HER TOWN.

THAT WOULD DISRUPT THE PREDETERMINED PROCESS OF THE ENTIRE SYSTEM!
IF I DID...!!
IF. YOU. DID.
YES, THAT WOULD CORRUPT THE VERY PURPOSE OF OUR EXISTENCE.
I'M GLAD YOU REMEMBER. I FEARED YOU MIGHT HAVE FORGOTTEN THAT LITTLE DETAIL.
WE CAUSE AIR AND WATER TO FLOW. WE MAKE THE SEASONS EXIST.
WIND AND RAIN, COLD AND HEAT, DRYNESS AND HUMIDITY.
WE MAKE THE ENTIRE SYSTEM CIRCULATE.
WE ALLOW THE HUMANS TO FARM, RAISE LIVESTOCK, GATHER TOGETHER AND SURVIVE.
THE HUMAN RACE SURVIVED BECAUSE OF OUR SYSTEM.

UNFORTUNATELY, NO SYSTEM IS PERFECT. ERRORS CREEP IN AND CAUSE VARIOUS NATURAL DISASTERS.
THOSE ARE UNAVOIDABLE SACRIFICES.
WE KILL A SMALL NUMBER OF HUMANS, RELATIVELY SPEAKING, IN ORDER TO SAVE THE WHOLE.
WE'VE KILLED COUNTLESS PEOPLE THOUGH.
THAT TOWN WILL BE NO DIFFERENT.
IF IT SOMEHOW BECOMES DIFFERENT... IF YOU ACT DIFFERENT... THEN, YOU ARE NOT WORTHY.
...
YOU GUARANTEED ME THAT YOU WOULDN'T MANIPULATE PEOPLE'S LIVES BASED ON PERSONAL EMOTIONS.
YOU MAY USE YOUR POWER ON THE HUMANS ONLY IF THEY OBSTRUCT THE PERFORMANCE OF YOUR DUTIES AS THE WATER KING.
ROLLING AROUND IN THE SACK WITH A YOUNG GIRL IS IRRELEVANT TO YOUR DUTIES.
SQUIRM
SO, JUST CONTINUE DOING AS YOU HAVE BEEN ALL ALONG.

IF YOU REFUSE, DON'T EXPECT ME TO DO NOTHING.
DO YOU WISH TO KILL MY BODY SO BADLY?
YOU HATE ME THAT MUCH?
DON'T MAKE ME OUT TO BE SOME JEALOUS GUY.
AS FOR ANO... SHE IS BULLHEADED AND CAN ONLY THINK ABOUT HER OWN WANTS.
SHE JUST WANTS TO PULL YOU COMPLETELY INTO MARGOT.
AS FOR ME, I ALWAYS LOOK AT THE BIG PICTURE.
YOUR REMAINING HUMANITY MAKES THE SYSTEM LESS STABLE.
THAT'S NOT TRUE!
ON TOP OF IT ALL, YOU BRING IN SOME FOOL WOMAN WHO DOESN'T HELP MATTERS.

I TOLD YOU, I'M JUST PLAYING AROUND WITH HER!
NO, ANO!
HOW COULD I BE SERIOUS ABOUT PLAYING HOUSE WITH A HUMAN GIRL?
DON'T WORRY ABOUT IT.
SO, JUST LEAVE THEM ALONE!
SEE? YOU'RE GETTING RILED UP AGAIN OVER AN INSIGNIFICANT REGION, ONE OF MANY YOU MUST SUPERVISE.
YOU'RE A GOD NOW!
NEVER FORGET THAT!
UGH...

EVEN IF I DON'T INVOLVE MYSELF, IF MARGOT DETERMINES THAT THE MORTAL WOMAN IS AN UNSTABLE FACTOR...
...THEN, SHE WILL MOST CERTAINLY NOT LEAVE YOUR WIFE ALONE.
YOU WANTED TO HIDE HER FROM MARGOT, RIGHT?
YOU'RE TRYING TOO HARD.
HONESTLY, THIS TASK SHOULD BE EASIER THAN KILLING AN INSECT.
REMEMBER. MARGOT AND I ARE WATCHING.
P-ZZZT
...
HAA
HAA

YOU'LL BE WATCHING?
WHATEVER.
YOU'RE TRYING TO USE MY HUMAN EMOTIONS TO DESTABILIZE THE SYSTEM...
YOU'RE JUST TRYING TO AGITATE ME AND CAUSE ME TO LOSE MY NERVE AS THE WATER KING.
...AND FORCE ME GIVE UP MY BODY OF MY OWN ACCORD.
LORD GANOK!
I LOOKED AT THE PREDICTION DATA FOR THE CURRENT RAINY SEASON.
WHY WAS THERE A SUDDEN CHANGE?
NOTHING HAS CHANGED.
LORD GANOK...
THIS IS WHAT WE'VE ALWAYS DONE. NOTHING HAS CHANGED.
JUST MAKE SURE SHE NEVER FINDS OUT.
PARDON?

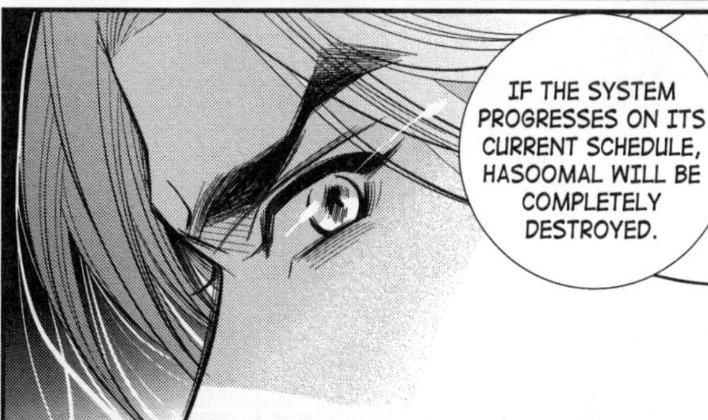
IF THE SYSTEM PROGRESSES ON ITS CURRENT SCHEDULE, HASOOMAL WILL BE COMPLETELY DESTROYED.
JUST MAKE SURE SHE NEVER FINDS OUT.

...
WE MUST BRING HER BACK.
WHERE IS SHE RIGHT NOW?
SHE WANTED TO TAKE CARE OF SOMETHING. SHE WENT INTO TOWN.
WHATEVER. YOU'RE CONSIDERED GOOD-LOOKING HERE. YOU'RE PROBABLY JUST A HICK IN A BIG CITY.
CITY PEOPLE ARE TOUGH, SO YOU HAVE TO BE TOUGH YOURSELF, NARIGA.
ACTUALLY, I'M CONSIDERED FAIRLY GOOD-LOOKING IN THE CITY, TOO
I MADE SO MANY GIRLS CRY WHILE STUDYING THERE.
I'LL BE OKAY. I'M SMART AND GOOD-LOOKING. I'M USED TO BEING ENVIED.
HAHA...
WHATEVER! AT LEAST, UNFOUNDED CONFIDENCE IS BETTER THAN LACKING SELF ESTEEM!

MAKE SURE YOU SUCCEED, OKAY?
FORGET WHAT I SAID BEFORE. FIND YOURSELF A PRETTY CITY GIRL AND LIVE PROUDLY.
NO, I CAN'T DO THAT.
...
IT'S NOT THAT I DON'T WANT TO, BUT I DON'T THINK I CAN.
I THOUGHT I COULD GET OVER YOU, BUT I WAS WRONG.
I KNOW IT DOESN'T MAKE SENSE, BUT I JUST CAN'T.
I DECIDED NOT TO TRUST MY HEART ANYMORE.
IT DOESN'T LISTEN TO ME ANYWAY. THERE'S NOTHING MORE I CAN DO.
NARIGA...
IF YOU EVER NEED ME...
...YOU KNOW WHERE TO FIND ME.

DID WE AGREE YET THAT WE'RE EVEN?
NO.
GOOD, BECAUSE I'M GOING TO BE THE BIGGER FOOL.
THE QUEEN IS IN TOWN?
I NEED TO TELL YOU SOMETHING.
YOU HIGHNESS, THE WATER KING!
THEN, WHERE IS SHE?
WHAT?
I HAVEN'T SEEN HER.
NERVOUS

I KEPT WATCH OVER HER BECAUSE I FEARED IMPROPRIETY.
I'M TELLING YOU THIS OUT OF MY LOYALTY TO YOU, SO PLEASE LOOK KINDLY UPON ME.
...
THE QUEEN IS...
!

ONE LAST TIME.
NO, ANO...
I'M JUST PLAYING...
...WITH THAT GIRL.

WOONG
CLENCH

JUST AS I PREDICTED. THIS IS AN UNUSUAL BRAIN PATTERN.
LORD GANOK...
HE SEARCHED FOR YOU IN YOUR HOMETOWN. HE'S BEEN ACTING STRANGE EVER SINCE HIS RETURN.
...
GANOK?

I KEPT WAITING, BUT YOU NEVER CAME TO DINNER.
YOU ALWAYS EAT WITH ME UNLESS SOMETHING IS WRONG.
AHH!

H-HOLD ON.
WHY ARE YOU BEING SO...
AHHH!
...!
W-WAIT. HOLD ON.
I NEVER SAID NO, SO WHY...?!

AHH!
KREEK
KREEK
AHH UGH!
KREEK
KREEK
THAT HURTS...
KREEK
AAH!
KREEK
AHHH!
KREEK

YOU'RE TRULY AWFUL.
HE SEEMS STRANGE.
IT FEELS LIKE HE JUST WANTS TO TAKE FROM ME.
WHY?
AS LONG AS YOU STAY WITH ME...
AHH...

...I DON'T NEED ANYTHING ELSE. I JUST NEED YOU.
...!
I WON'T LET YOU GO. EVER.
I'LL FOLD YOU UP AND CARRY YOU IN MY POCKET IF I MUST.
YOU'RE MINE.
DO AS I SAY.
GO BACK TO YOUR ROOM. AND DON'T LEAVE THE CASTLE FOR THE NEXT FEW DAYS.
WHY ARE YOU BEING THIS WAY?
SLAM

HAA
HAA
SOMETHING'S...
...UP.
MARGOT...
MARGOT!
OUCH
PLOP

THIS IS THE FIRST TIME YOU INITIATED THE LINK YOURSELF.
WHAT DO YOU WISH?
DID SOMETHING HAPPEN TO GANOK?
SOMETHING FEELS WRONG.
WELL, YOU WOULD'VE LEARNED THIS INFORMATION EVENTUALLY, SO...

SOOYI...
YOUR HOMETOWN
HASOOMAL...
...WILL BE
DESTROYED BY
A FLOOD
IN 2 DAYS.
WHAT...?
DID YOU NOT
HEAR ME?
I'LL REPEAT IT THEN.
YOUR HOMETOWN
HASOOMAL
WILL BE...
WHY?!
...
WHY...
WHY?!!!
WHY ASK?
NATURAL
DISASTERS DO NOT
REQUIRE A REASON.

NATURAL... DISASTER?
A FLOOD? BUT, THE WATER KING...
AS EXPECTED, DO YOU INTEND TO...?
WHAT? DO I INTEND TO WHAT?
WILL YOU TRY TO INFLUENCE GANOK, AS I EXPECT?
WELL...
NO HUMAN BEING CAN JUST SIT IDLY BY WHILE HER HOMETOWN AND FAMILY ARE ABOUT TO DIE!
NO HUMAN...
AS EXPECTED.
ARE YOU TESTING ME?
AHHHK!
MARGOT! MARGOT!
REEL

HAA
HAA
WHY...
...!
GANOK!
LISTEN TO ME!
WE NEED TO TALK!
...
WHAT ARE YOU DOING? I TOLD YOU TO STAY IN YOUR ROOM.
THIS IS IMPORTANT!

THERE WILL BE TIMES WHEN I DON'T WISH TO TALK TO YOU AT ALL.
REEL
AH...
YOU'RE ACTING STRANGE.
...!
HE SEARCHED FOR YOU IN YOUR HOMETOWN.
NO WAY...
GANOK...
YOU CAME TO TOWN EARLIER?
DID YOU... SEE ME?

FORGET IT. DON'T SAY ANYTHING MORE.
BUT, GANOK!
SLAM
I WANT TO CHOKE THE LIFE FROM YOU, BUT I'M RESISTING.
I KNOW IN MY HEAD...
...YOU TWO GREW UP TOGETHER. HE WAS YOUR FIRST.
HE IS A PART OF YOUR LIFE THAT CAN NEVER BE CUT OUT. I'M SURE YOU FELT CONFUSED WHEN YOU SAID YOUR FAREWELLS.
SO, IT PISSES ME OFF THAT WHAT I SAW UPSETS ME THIS MUCH.

HE'S ANGRY...
IS THIS WHY YOU PLAN TO FLOOD HASOOMAL?
WHAT?!
I MADE HIM... ANGRY...
ARE YOU PUNISHING ME BECAUSE YOU'RE ANGRY?

AAAAACK!
FROOM
HOW DID YOU FIND OUT?
HAA
HAA
IS IT TRUE? YOU PLAN ON DESTROYING MY TOWN?
I ASKED YOU, HOW DID YOU LEARN THIS INFORMATION?!

DIOR DIDN'T TELL YOU, I'M SURE OF IT. AND YOU COULDN'T HAVE ACCESSED THE SYSTEM YOURSELF...
BUT...
YOU!
KYAAA
DID YOU LINK UP WITH MARGOT?
YES, I DID. WHAT ABOUT IT?!
MARGOT TELLS ME THINGS YOU NEVER WILL!
YOU'RE HURTING ME!
DID YOU LINK UP WITH MARGOT?!

IF MARGOT DETERMINES THAT THE MORTAL WOMAN IS AN UNSTABLE FACTOR...
I TOLD YOU NEVER TO GO INSIDE THE CHAMBER! WHY DIDN'T YOU LISTEN TO ME?!
...SHE WILL MOST CERTAINLY NOT LEAVE YOUR WIFE ALONE.
I WAS WORRIED ABOUT YOU!
HONESTLY, THIS TASK SHOULD BE EASIER THAN KILLING A INSECT.
IS MY KNOWING SO BAD? WHAT'S SO AWFUL ABOUT ME KNOWING MORE ABOUT YOU?
...!!
AAAACK!!

UGH...
HAA
HAA

THERE EXIST THINGS YOU SHOULD NEVER KNOW!
WHY ARE YOU SO FEARLESS, YOU LITTLE BRAT?!
AAACK...
DIOR! PAINKILLER!
SEEING YOUR REACTION, I GUESS IT'S ALL TRUE.
...
YOU TRULY INTEND TO WIPE OUT HASOOMAL.
LISTEN, KIDDO...
FOR A MOMENT, I FORGOT... MY BODY IS NOT MY OWN.
I'M JUST ONE OF YOUR MANY POSSESSIONS.

BUT, I'M THE ONE WHO MADE A MISTAKE!
PLEASE, JUST PUNISH ME INSTEAD!
WHY ARE YOU TAKING YOUR VENGEANCE OUT ON THEM?
SHUT UP! THIS NEEDS TO BE TREATED!
THIS WON'T HURT IF YOU...
TAP
KLANG
YOU CAN RIP OUT ALL 10 FINGERNAILS IF THAT WILL QUENCH YOUR ANGER!
STOP TALKING NONSENSE! DON'T BE FOOLISH!

I'LL TAKE ALL OF THE PUNISHMENT!
I KNOW I MESSED UP. I WAS WRONG!
PLEASE, JUST SPARE MY TOWN!
IT CAN'T BE CHANGED.
WHY... CAN'T IT CHANGE?
YOU ARE... THE WATER KING.
YOU COMMAND THE WATER ANY WAY YOU PLEASE.

I'M SORRY.
I'M SORRY.
I'M SORRY...!
HOWEVER...
I'M VERY SORRY...!
...I...
..PLEASE.
PLEASE, I'LL BEG ON MY KNEES.
I'LL DO WHATEVER YOU TELL ME TO DO!
YOU CAN DO ANYTHING YOU WANT TO ME! ANYTHING!
JUST PLEASE...
PLEASE... PLEASE...
DON'T DO IT...
THIS FEELING...
THIS FEELING..

MY HEART ITSELF FEELS LIKE ITS BLEEDING. I CAN FEEL EVERY DROP.
I'LL CONSIDER IT AS A MISTAKE, BUT...
I FEEL AS IF...
...MY HEART JUST EXPLODED.
I FEEL LIKE IT HAS SHATTERED INTO COUNTLESS SHARDS...
...SCRAPING AT ME BENEATH MY RIBS.
THE NEXT TIME I SEE YOU KISS ANOTHER MAN, I'LL SHRED HIM TO PIECES.
AND STOP COMPLAINING ABOUT HASOOMAL.
THAT TOWN'S DESTRUCTION IS NOT BECAUSE OF THE KISS.

YOU MAY BE TEMPTED TO THINK I'M JUST A HUMAN MAN, BECAUSE I LET YOU INFLUENCE ME.
BUT, I'M NOT PETTY ENOUGH TO WIPE OUT A TOWN OUT OF JEALOUSY.
THE WATER KING ISN'T THAT PATHETIC.
I CAN'T BELIEVE I FEEL THIS AWFUL...
...JUST LIKE WHEN I WAS A HUMAN BEING.
THEN, WHY? WHY ARE YOU DOING IT?!
I JUST WANTED TO KEEP HER LIKE A TREASURE HIDDEN INSIDE MY POCKET.
THAT WAY, NEITHER SHE NOR I WOULD GET HURT.
I TOLD YOU, YOU HAVE NO RIGHT TO KNOW!
SO HOW...?!
HOW DO YOU HAVE THIS ABILITY TO MAKE ME FEEL SO MISERABLE?
HOW FAR DO YOU PLAN ON TESTING ME?!

HAAA
HAAA

HASOOMAL WILL BE FLOODED.
THAT FACT WILL NOT CHANGE. SO...
...JUST CONCENTRATE ON SAVING YOUR OWN LIFE!

HEY!
STOP RIGHT THERE! WHERE...
HAA
REEL
I'M GOING TO THE TOWN.
I MUST CONVINCE THEM TO EVACUATE.
...

FINE. GO DOWN AND TELL THEM TO ESCAPE.
I'LL GRANT YOU THAT MUCH.
HOWEVER, DON'T GET DESPERATE!
IF YOUR PEOPLE REFUSE TO LISTEN, JUST GET YOUR FAMILY OUT.
YOU CAN'T SAVE EVERYONE.

HOW CAN THIS BE?!
HOW...
HOW COULD...
PLEASE, PACK ONLY THE NECESSITIES.
I NEED TO WARN THE HEAD ELDER, SO PEOPLE CAN START LEAVING AS QUICKLY AS POSSIBLE.
OKAY.
HAHA...
THANK YOU FOR YOUR GENEROUS HOSPITALITY.
WHAT DO YOU MEAN? FOR LOOGOO CITY'S AMBASSADOR, THIS MEAL MUST SEEM QUITE SIMPLE.
HASOOMAL WILL BECOME A CENTRAL REGION NOW.
IT WILL BE REWARDING TO SEE THIS TOWN FLOURISH.
INDEED, YOU WILL BECOME WEALTHIER THAN MOST NOBLEMEN IN LARGE CITIES.

YOU'RE TOO KIND.
I'LL NEED YOUR HELP.
I WON'T FORGET YOUR KINDNESS AFTER FORTUNE SMILES UPON ME.
TO LOOGOO CITY AND HASOOMAL!
I WILL COMPENSATE YOU GENEROUSLY.
HAHA
UM... SIR?
WHAT IS IT?
THE WATER QUEEN IS HERE.
AT THIS HOUR?
W-WHAT DID YOU JUST SAY?
THE AIN RIVER WILL OVERFLOW.
HASOOMAL WILL BE SUBMERGED.

THE AIN RIVER OVERFLOWS EVERY RAINY SEASON.
THIS FLOOD WILL BE FAR GREATER IN MAGNITUDE!
SO...!
...
I UNDERSTAND.
I'LL MEET WITH THE OTHER LEADERS AND INFORM THE PEOPLE.
WON'T IT BE TOO LATE?
IF WE MAKE A SUDDEN ANNOUNCEMENT, THE ENTIRE TOWN WILL FALL INTO PANIC AND CHAOS.
WE NEED TO ORGANIZE OUR PLANS FIRST.

IF YOU ATTEND THE MEETING, PEOPLE WILL JUST RAISE MORE QUESTIONS AND THINGS WILL BE DELAYED.
TRUST ME AND WAIT A LITTLE.
THE LIFE OF OUR PEOPLE IS AT RISK. I'LL TAKE CARE OF IT.
...
KLIK
WHAT WAS THAT ABOUT?
THIS TOWN WILL BE SUBMERGED?!
THAT... WILL NEVER HAPPEN.
I'LL MAKE SURE IT DOESN'T.
WHATEVER IT TAKES.
OH NO! I DOZED OFF. IS IT MORNING?

SIR?
OKAY, GOOD WORK.

RETURN TO THE PALACE RIGHT NOW.
WHEN WILL YOU GATHER THE TOWNS PEOPLE?

...?!

GO AND CONVINCE THE WATER KING TO HALT THE FLOOD.
DO WHATEVER YOU MUST.

WHAT ARE YOU TALKING ABOUT?
I SENT MY MEN TO YOUR FAMILY'S HOUSE.
HARSH TIMES CALL FOR HARSH MEASURES.
I'M KEEPING YOUR ENTIRE FAMILY IMPRISONED IN MY BASEMENT.
...!!
S-SIR...!
W-WHAT HAVE YOU DONE?
GO BACK AND FIX WHATEVER YOU DID WRONG!
WHY WOULD THE WATER KING WIPE OUT THIS TOWN?
YOU MUST'VE DONE SOMETHING WRONG!

DO YOU HONESTLY BELIEVE...
...I'M ANYTHING MORE THAN A PET TO HIM?
YOU MUST HAVE ANGERED HIM SOMEHOW!
YOU FOOL!
WHAT DO YOU EXPECT OF ME?!
HE'S A DEMON KING! HE WON'T BE SWAYED BY HIS HUMAN BEDMATE!
...
THE FLOOD WILL COME IN A DAY OR TWO!
I CAN'T BELIEVE YOU WASTED PRECIOUS TIME DOING THIS!!
FIND A WAY, MY QUEEN!
OR ELSE YOUR PRECIOUS FAMILY WILL DIE!!

OUR TOWN IS ABOUT TO BE SHOWERED BY UNTOLD WEALTH!
SACRIFICING A GIRL TO THE DEMON KING SHOULD'VE EARNED US HIS FAVOR!
YOU JUST NEED TO TRY HARDER!
WHAT DID YOU DO TO MALIGN THIS TOWN SO BADLY?
DO SOMETHING!
YOU'RE THE WATER KING'S WOMAN.
HOW COULD YOU BE SO STUPID...
YOU... HAVE NO IDEA...
HAA
HAA

IS ANYONE OUT THERE?!
THUD
SIR!
H-HELP!
FREEZE!
WHAT ARE YOU DOING? SAVE ME!
HALT
WHOSE ORDERS DO YOU THINK YOU SHOULD OBEY?
HIS OR MINE?

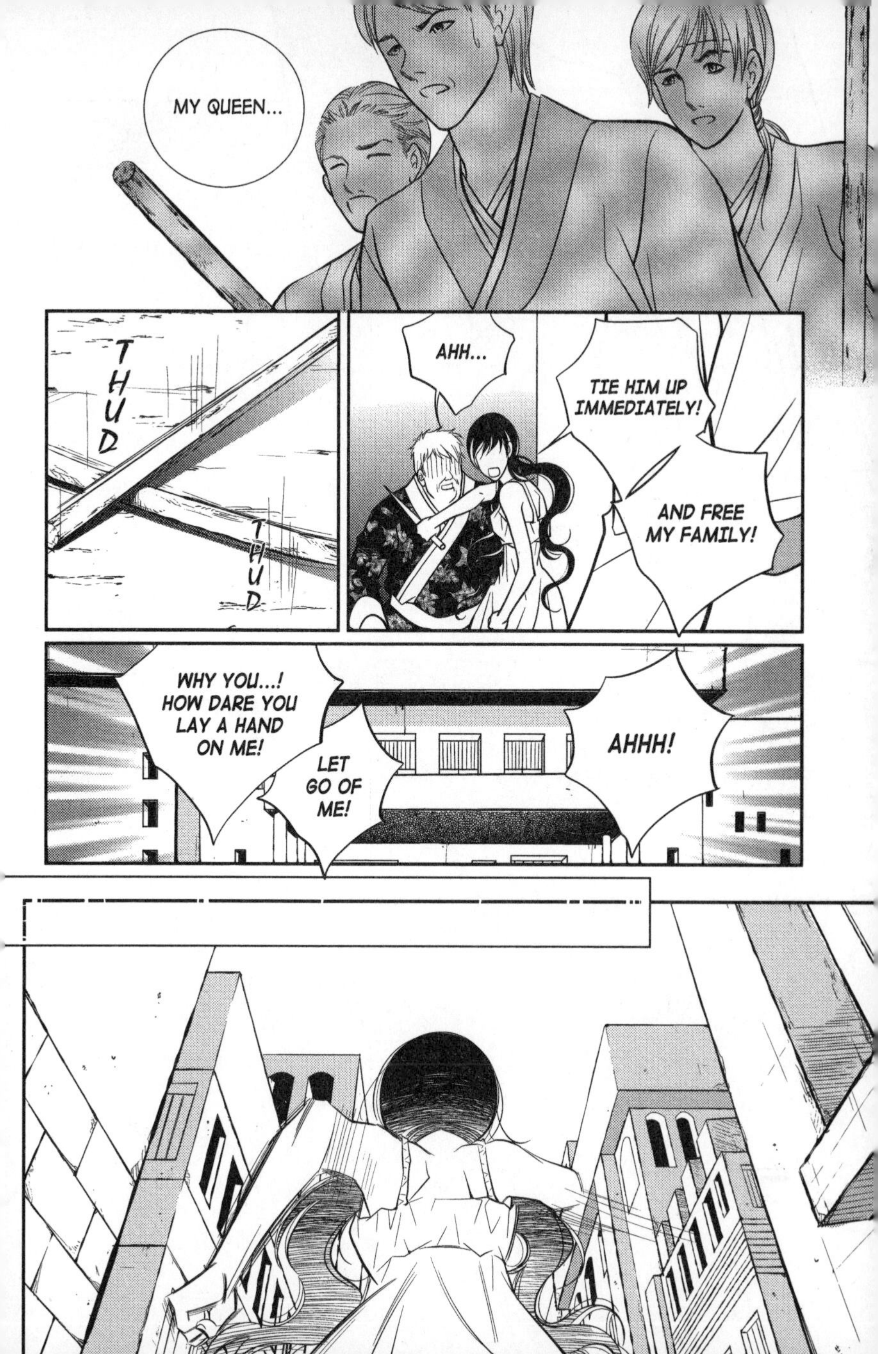
MY QUEEN...
THUD
THUD
AHH...
TIE HIM UP IMMEDIATELY!
AND FREE MY FAMILY!
AHHH!
WHY YOU...! HOW DARE YOU LAY A HAND ON ME!
LET GO OF ME!

EVERYONE! LISTEN TO ME!
THE WATER QUEEN...
THE WATER QUEEN?
MUMBLE
EVERYONE, GO HOME! TAKE YOUR FAMILIES UP THE MOUNTAIN!
YOU HAVE NO TIME TO PACK! YOU MUST SAVE YOURSELVES! HURRY!

W-WHAT DO YOU MEAN? WHERE'S THE HEAD ELDER?
THAT'S NOT IMPORTANT RIGHT NOW!
THIS IS RIDICULOUS. YOU CAN'T JUST COMMAND US TO ABANDON THE TOWN AND RUN!
LISTEN TO ME. PLEASE...
THIS TOWN WILL SOON BE DESTROYED!
WATCH YOUR MOUTH! HOW CAN YOU EXPECT US TO LEAVE THIS LAND?
WE'D BE PUNISHED!
YEAH. YEAH.
WE'VE PROTECTED THIS LAND FOR GENERATIONS.
IF WE LEAVE, WE CAN'T SURVIVE.
!
WE SUFFER FLOODS EVERY YEAR. PEOPLE DIE ALL THE TIME. THOSE WHO SURVIVE ALWAYS KEEP THE TOWN GOING.
THAT IS THE WILL OF THE GODS!
YEAH.
WE CAN'T LEAVE THIS TOWN. WE'LL BE PUNISHED FOR OUR LACK OF FAITH!
EVEN A FLOOD COMES FROM THE WILL OF THE GODS. WE MUST ENDURE IT AND PRAY FOR MERCY.
ANYONE WHO BELIEVES OTHERWISE DOESN'T DESERVE TO LIVE HERE!
WHAT?
ARE YOU SAYING YOU'LL DISOBEY THE WATER QUEEN'S ORDERS?

THEN, WILL YOU LEAVE TOWN?
IF IT'S THE WATER QUEEN'S ORDERS!
YOU'LL BE PUNISHED!
ONLY OLD PEOPLE LIKE YOU BELIEVE IN SUCH FOOLISHNESS!
WHAT?
NO, SOMETHING'S NOT RIGHT.
WHY WOULD THE WATER KING WISH TO DESTROY HIS WIFE'S HOMETOWN?
IS THIS THE WATER KING'S WRATH?
IS THAT IT? DID THE WATER QUEEN OFFEND HIM SOMEHOW?
WATCH YOUR MOUTH! HOW DARE YOU INSULT THE QUEEN?
THIS ISN'T THE TIME TO TAKE HER SIDE.
THIS TOWN IS ABOUT TO BE DESTROYED BECAUSE OF HER!
BEG HER FOR FORGIVENESS!
YOU'RE TRAITORS! JUST DIE!
MY QUEEN, I'LL FOLLOW YOU!
YOU'RE BEING PUNISHED BECAUSE OF YOUR LACK OF FAITH!
YOU WANT A PIECE OF ME?
DEAR GODS, PLEASE FORGIVE THEM!
COME AND GET ME!
KILL THEM!

REEL
EVERYONE, PLEASE!
SHUT UP... SHUT UP!
PLEASE JUST RUN!

GOGOGOGOO
!
REEL
IT'S SHAKING... UNDER MY FEET...
GOGOGOGOO
LOOK...
DROP
DROP
I FEEL A VIBRATION COMING FROM BEYOND THE MOUNTAIN.
DROP
KROOOM

I HELD OUT A LITTLE HOPE...
THAT HE WOULD AT LEAST WAIT UNTIL I WAS GONE.
!
KROOM
MAYBE WE SHOULD ALL JUST DIE TOGETHER...
...HERE.
AAACK
I'M STILL HERE.
I'M STILL HERE...
AAACK

KROOM

AAAAAAAACK
...
HUMM
...

KRRRRRNG
AH...
AHHH...
KRNG

SHWAAAA
WHY DID YOU SAVE ME? WHY?
I WANTED TO BE WASHED AWAY WITH THEM. SO WHY?!!
...
UGH...
UGH...
AAAAAAAAAH

HAA
HAA

UGH...
UGH...
SPLASH
SPLASH
THIS ALL MUST BE JUST A NIGHTMARE, RIGHT? LEAH!!
LEAH?

AH...
D-DAD...
MOM...
AH...
AAAACK...
CHEE...
BABY...
LOUIE...

AAAAAAAAH
KLANG
KLANG
AAAACK

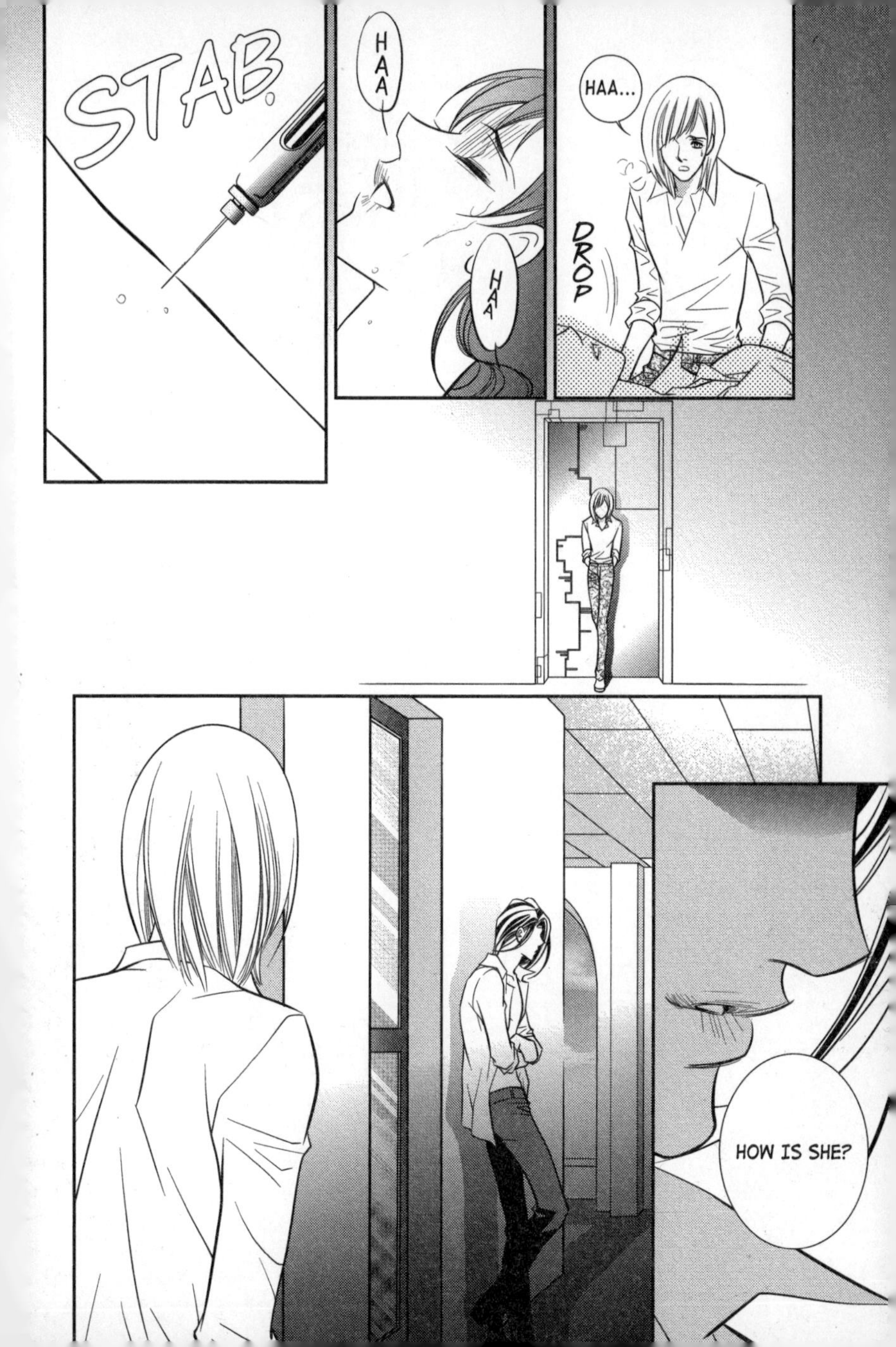
STAB
HAA
HAA
HAA...
DROP
HOW IS SHE?

I'M USING AS MUCH SEDATIVES AS SHE CAN TOLERATE.
DON'T ENTER.
EVEN THOUGH DAYS HAVE PASSED, SHE STILL TRIES TO BITE AND SCRATCH YOU. SOOYI LOSES HER MIND EVERY TIME SHE SEES YOU.
SHE KEEPS HURTING HERSELF. I CAN'T REMOVE THE SHACKLES...
To be continued in volume

Give to the Heart

Give to the Heart

6

WANN